Salvino

The Whale Who Wanted to be Small

By Gill McBarnet

Ruwanga Trading

Also published by Ruwanga Trading Inc:
The Wonderful Journey
A Whale's Tale
The Pink Parrot
Fountain of Fire
The Shark Who Learned a Lesson
The Goodnight Gecko
Gecko Hide And Seek
The Brave Little Turtle
The Gift of Aloha

Book Orders and Enquires:
Booklines, Hawaii Ltd.,
94-527 Puahi Street,
Waipahu, Hi 96797

Printed and Bound in China
under direction of:
Phoenix Offset

ISBN 0-9615102-O-X

For Eddie and Willie

In the sparkling blue ocean around the Hawaiian islands there once lived a whale who wanted to be small. Although she was only a baby whale, Kanani was already much much bigger than any of her friends. This made her rather shy.

"Oh dear" she would often say. "If only I were not so big and clumsy. I wish I was small like my friends."

One day Iwalani the seabird cried out to Kanani. "The whale hunters are coming. You must hide. Quick, quick. Go and hide!"

"What shall I do? Where can I hide? Is there any place big enough for me to hide?" cried Kanani.

Tako the octopus came to help her. "Squeeze this ink into the water in front of you and the whale hunters will not be able to see you." The octopus squeezed some of the ink into the water.

None of the other sea creatures could see him behind his cloud of black ink.

"Now you try" said Tako.

When Kanani tried to hide behind her cloud of ink it stung her eyes and, anyway, there was not enough ink to cover her big body.

"I have a better idea" said Kilila the spotted eel. "Follow me into my cave. The whale hunters will not find you in here." And with that Kilila slipped into his rocky cave.

None of his friends could see him because it was dark and shadowy inside the cave.

Kanani wriggled and wriggled and
tried to push her way through the
rocks.

But only the tip of her nose fitted,
and the rest of her that did not fit
looked just like a whale trying to
wriggle into a cave.

A sweet voice spoke up from a nearby rock. It was Leilani the sea anemone.

"Why not cover yourself with flowers? That way, the whale hunters will think you are anemones and they will not disturb you."

"What a clever way to hide. You look just like a flower!" laughed Kanani.

Kanani saw a lei seller on the beach and she bought as many leis as she could carry. She swam back to the rocks where the anemones lived.

The anemones swayed their feelers gracefully from side to side like hula dancers.

Kanani covered herself with leis and she moved her body from side to side like the anemones.

But no matter how much she swayed from side to side she still looked like a whale pretending to be anemones.

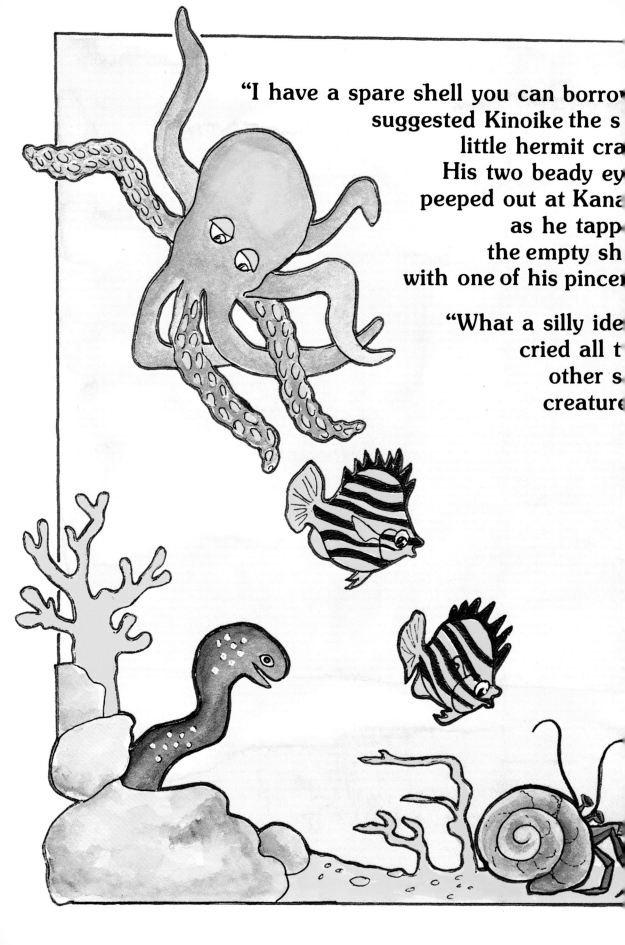

"I have a spare shell you can borrow,"
suggested Kinoike the s—
little hermit cra—
His two beady ey—
peeped out at Kana—
as he tapp—
the empty sh—
with one of his pincer—

"What a silly ide—
cried all t—
other s—
creature—

"Thanks all the same Kinoike" said Kanani. "But if I cannot fit into Kilila the eel's cave, how would I be able to hide in that tiny shell?"

Olu the turtle tried to help.

"Swim to the bottom of the ocean and lie down in the sea grass. The whale hunters will think you are a rock and they will sail over you in their boat."

Olu tucked her head and flippers into her shell so that she looked like a rock at the bottom of the ocean.

Kanani lay very still in the sea grass and made herself as small as she could.

But she was not able to tuck in her big flippers or her long tail, so she looked like a whale pretending to be a rock.

"Oh dear" cried Kanani. "I have tried everything but there is no place big enough for me to hide. How I wish I was small, but I am so BIG I can be seen from miles away. And now the whale hunters are going to catch me!"

Poor Kanani sobbed as if her heart would break and great big whale sized tears splashed down her cheeks.

Just then there was a loud humming sound, and all the other sea creatures moved aside as Kapunekane the great big grandfather whale swam up to Kanani.

"Well, well, well, my dear little Kanani. Why are you crying?" asked grandfather whale in his deep gentle voice.

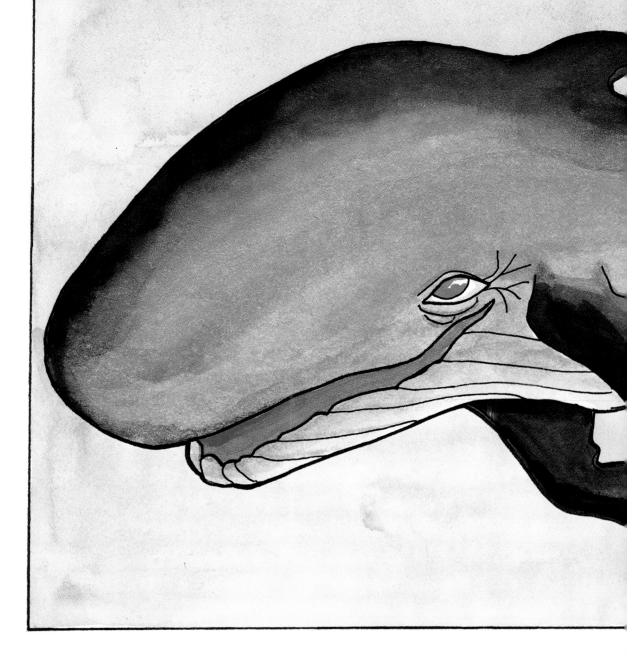

"I am crying because I want to be small so that the whale hunters will not catch me. You are so old and clever Kapunekane. Please tell me how I can make myself small like my friends" sobbed Kanani.

"My little Kanani" chuckled her grandfather. "You must not be afraid. Men stopped hunting whales around here a long time ago. Boats now carry friendly people who like to watch us swimming in the ocean. The people carry cameras and they take pictures of us to show their friends. They tell stories of how they have seen the biggest creatures in the whole wide world."

"Look at me. I love being big!" shouted Kapunekane as he leapt out of the water.

The water foamed and splashed.

"You see?" winked grandfather. "They have not hurt me. Now you try."

Kanani lifted her head out of the foaming water and a little boy shouted "Oh look, a baby whale!" All the people cheered and Kanani's eyes shone with pride.

"Are you happy now?" asked Kapunekane.

"Yes grandfather" Kanani replied. "But there is just one thing …"

"You have shown me how nice it is to be BIG so I do not want to be small anymore. Now I want to be the biggest whale in the whole wide world!"

THE

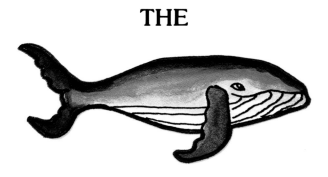

END

HUMPBACK WHALES

Kanani is a member
of the Humpback Whale family.

Male Humpbacks grow to a maximum length of 58 feet and females to a maximum of 62 feet – about the length of a city bus.

Both male and female adults can weigh as much as 53 tons.

Baby Humpbacks are about 15 feet long and they weigh 1.5 tons at birth – about the same weight as an automobile.

Humpback Whales are the most playful of all the great whales, and they love to leap and somersault about in the ocean.

The time to see Humpbacks in Hawaii is from December to April. After April they migrate to their polar feeding grounds in search of food.